Karen

**Look for these
and other books about Karen
in the
Baby-sitters Little Sister series:**

Little Sister

Karen's Turkey Day

Ann M. Martin

Illustrations by Susan Tang

A
LITTLE APPLE
PAPERBACK

SCHOLASTIC INC.
New York Toronto London Auckland Sydney

No part of this publication may be reproduced in whole or in part, or stored in a retrieval system, or transmitted in any form or by any means, electronic, mechanical, photocopying, recording, or otherwise, without written permission of the publisher. For information regarding permission, write to Scholastic Inc., 555 Broadway, New York, NY 10012.

ISBN 0-590-26024-3

12 11 10 9 8 7 6 5 4 3 2 1   5 6 7 8 9/9 0/0

Printed in the U.S.A.   40

First Scholastic printing, November 1995

The author gratefully acknowledges
Stephanie Calmenson
for her help
with this book.

Karen's Turkey Day

1

The Little House

"See you tomorrow!" I called to my friend Nancy Dawes.

I raced from the school bus to the little house. Mommy was waiting at the door with open arms. Midgie, our dog, came running outside. (Rocky, our cat, just flicked his tail and watched us from inside.)

"I am home," I said.

"I am so happy to see you!" she said.

I knew she really was, too. You see, when I said I was home, I did not mean I was home from just one day of school. I was also home from one whole month at the big house. I woke up in the morning at the big house. I would go to sleep that night at the little house. (Later I will tell you why I have two houses.)

My name is Karen Brewer. I am seven years old. I have blonde hair, blue eyes, and a bunch of freckles. I wear glasses, too. I even have two pairs. I wear my blue pair for reading. I wear my pink pair the rest of the time.

"Where is Andrew?" I asked. Andrew is my little brother. He is four going on five. He usually gets home from school before I do.

"He will be home any minute," Mommy replied. "His carpool had to make an extra stop today. Why don't you go wash up? I will make a snack for you and your brother."

The first thing I did when I got to my room was give my stuffed cat, Goosie, a big hug.

"How have you been, Goosie?" I asked. "Moosie told me to say hi to you." (Moosie is my other stuffed cat. He lives at the big house.)

I checked on my dolls. Then I made sure Emily Junior's cage was ready for her. Emily Junior is my pet rat. She lives wherever I do. Someone from the big house was supposed to drop her off later in the afternoon.

I washed up, then ran downstairs for my snack. Just as I was sitting down, Andrew walked in.

"Hi, Mommy! Hi, Karen!" he said. He gave Mommy a big hug and a kiss. "Look what I made at school today. My teacher says Thanksgiving will be here soon."

Andrew put a paper pilgrim's hat on his head. Thanksgiving seemed like a long time away. But it really was not. Today was the first day of November. Thanksgiving was the last Thursday of the month. That was just four weeks away. Hooray! I love Thanksgiving.

After our snack, I went upstairs to do my homework. When I finished, I helped Mommy fix dinner.

"I think Seth might be late tonight," said Mommy. "He is already getting extra orders for the holidays. He will probably have to work late nights and every weekend right up until Christmas."

Seth is my stepfather. He is super nice. He has his own carpentry shop downtown in Stoneybrook.

At six o'clock, Seth called. Mommy was right. Seth had to work late. He said he would not be home for at least another hour. He wanted us to go ahead and eat without him.

It was too bad he was not home to have dinner with us. Mommy and I had made very delicious hamburgers with green beans and mashed potatoes. It was also too bad he was not home when Granny and Grandad called from Nebraska.

Granny and Grandad are Seth's mother and father. I once visited them all by myself. I flew there on an airplane. Another time my whole family visited them when Grandad was sick.

Mommy, Andrew, and I took turns talking on the phone. When we hung up, I was worried. Granny and Grandad sounded a little bit lonely. They had promised to call back in a couple of days. I was glad. Maybe they would sound happier then.

2

The Reason for
Two Houses

Now I am going to tell you why Andrew and I have two houses.

When I was really little, we lived with Mommy and Daddy in one house in Stoneybrook, Connecticut. Then Mommy and Daddy started fighting a lot. They said they loved Andrew and me very much. But they could not get along with each other anymore. So Mommy and Daddy got a divorce.

After the divorce, Mommy moved with my brother and me to the little house. (It is not too far away from the big house.)

Mommy met Seth and they got married. That is how Seth became my stepfather. The people who live at the little house are Mommy, Seth, Andrew, and me. The pets are Midgie, Rocky, Emily Junior, and Bob (Andrew's hermit crab). (Andrew and I switch houses every month. One month we live at the little house, the next month at the big house.)

Daddy stayed at the big house after the divorce. (It is the house he grew up in.) He met someone new, too. Her name is Elizabeth and she and Daddy got married. That is how Elizabeth became my stepmother. Elizabeth was married once before and has four children. They are my stepsister and stepbrothers. Kristy is thirteen and the best stepsister ever. David Michael is seven, like me. And Sam and Charlie are so old they are in high school.

I have one other sister. Remember I told you I have a pet rat named Emily Junior? Well, I named her after Emily Michelle. She is two and a half and I love her a lot. Daddy and Elizabeth adopted her from a faraway country called Vietnam.

I also have a very wonderful stepgrandmother. Nanny is Elizabeth's mother. She came to live at the big house to help take care of Emily. But really she helps take care of everyone.

There are pets at the big house, too. They are Shannon, who is David Michael's big Bernese mountain dog puppy; Boo-Boo, who is Daddy's cranky old cat; Crystal Light the Second, who is my goldfish; and Goldfishie, who is Andrew's you-know-what. Oh, yes. Emily Junior and Bob live at the big house whenever Andrew and I are there.

Guess what. I have special names for my brother and me. I call us Andrew Two-Two and Karen Two-Two. (I thought of those names after my teacher, Ms. Colman, read a book to our class. It was called *Jacob Two-Two Meets the Hooded Fang*.) I call us those names because we have two of so many things. We have two mommies and two daddies, two houses and two families, two cats and two dogs. We each have two sets of toys, and clothes, and books — one set at each house. I have two bicycles. Andrew has two tricycles. You already know about my two stuffed cats, Goosie and Moosie. I have two pieces of Tickly, my special blanket. I even have two best friends. Nancy Dawes lives next door to Mommy's house. Hannie Papadakis lives across the street and one house down from Daddy's house. (Nancy, Hannie, and I call ourselves the Three Musketeers. That is because we like to do everything together. We are even in the same second-grade class at Stoneybrook Academy.)

That is my story. Now you know why I have two houses.

3

The Surprise

Just before dinner on Thursday Seth called to say he would be late again. That made two nights in a row. But this time he was only going to be a little bit late.

"Can we wait for Seth?" I asked. "It is more fun when we all eat together."

"I agree," said Mommy. "And Seth and I have a surprise for you kids. We want to tell you together."

"Can't you tell us now?" I asked. "When Seth comes home, you can tell us again."

"But it will not be a surprise the second

time you hear it," said Mommy.

"We will act surprised. I promise. Tell us now, Mommy, please," I said.

Mommy said we had to wait. It was not easy. Dinner was already cooked. The table was already set. Waiting was the only thing left to do.

Finally Seth came home. The minute he walked through the door, Andrew and I shouted, "Tell us our surprise!"

First Seth wanted to take off his jacket. He wanted to wash his hands. Then Mommy and Seth wanted us to sit down at the table. They wanted to serve the food before it got cold. Finally they were ready to tell us their news.

"It is a Thanksgiving surprise," said Seth. "This year we are going to spend our holiday weekend in New York City."

"Yippee!" Andrew and I shouted. This was great news! We once went to New York at Christmastime. It was so much fun.

"We are going to stay in a hotel along

the parade route," said Mommy. "That way we can watch the Macy's Thanksgiving Day parade from our windows."

"That is so cool," I said.

"We have already made reservations to eat a special Thanksgiving dinner in a restaurant," said Seth.

"There will be time to do lots of other things," said Mommy. "We can go shopping, visit a museum, go to the zoo."

"Can we go to the place where there are stars?" asked Andrew.

"You mean Broadway?" asked Seth. "It may be hard to get show tickets on a holiday weekend."

"No. Not people stars," said Andrew. "Sky stars."

Mommy and Seth looked puzzled.

"I know the place he means," I said. "Andrew wants to go to the planetarium."

"That's it. The plabetarum," said Andrew.

"That is a very good idea," said Mommy.

"The planetarium is part of the Museum of Natural History. We can make that our museum trip."

"Will there be time for me to see Maxie?" I asked.

Maxie Medvin is my New York City pen pal. She is very nice.

"I don't see why not," said Mommy. "She can join us on one of our outings."

"Why don't you kids make a list of the things you would like to do? We will try to fit in as many as we can," said Seth.

I was so excited I had trouble eating dinner. As soon as we were excused, Andrew and I went upstairs to start our list. Thanksgiving was exactly four weeks away. We could hardly wait.

4

Show and Share

I was glad the next day was Friday. Friday is one of our Show and Share days at school. I wished it were time already. But the day had just started. There were other things to do.

"Karen, would you like to take attendance this morning?" asked Ms. Colman.

"Sure!" I replied.

Taking attendance is an important job. I like doing important jobs for Ms. Colman. Ms. Colman is a gigundoly wonderful teacher. She makes school interesting and

15

fun. And she is always nice. When I call out in class, Ms. Colman does not get angry. She just reminds me to use my indoor voice and to raise my hand.

I stood up and started checking off names in the attendance book. I put a check next to my name first. Then I checked off Hannie and Nancy because they are my best friends. They sit together at the back of the room. I used to sit with them until I got my glasses. Then Ms. Colman moved me to the front of the room with the other glasses wearers. Ms. Colman says we can see better up front. I checked off the other glasses wearers. They are Natalie Springer and Ricky Torres. (Ricky is my pretend husband. We got married on the playground at recess one afternoon.)

I checked off Addie Sydney. (She was busy putting turkey and pumpkin stickers on her wheelchair tray.) I checked off Pamela Harding, my best enemy, and her friends, Jannie Gilbert and Leslie Morris. I checked off the twins, Terri and Tammy

16

Barkan. I checked off Bobby Gianelli. (He used to be a bully, but he is not so much of a bully anymore.) I checked off Audrey Green and Hank Reubens.

I made a few more checks, then handed the book to Ms. Colman. It was a good day. Everyone was in school. That meant everyone would get to hear my news.

"Is it time for Show and Share now?" I asked.

"Not yet," replied Ms. Colman. "First I would like to talk about the next big holiday coming up."

"Thanksgiving!" I called. "That is what I want to talk about, too."

"But Karen, you forgot to raise your hand. And you forgot to use your indoor voice," said Ms. Colman.

Oops. I usually forget when I am excited. And I was very excited about sharing my news.

"Sorry," I replied.

"I would like to start a list of things we have to be thankful for," said Ms. Colman.

"We can add to the list any time we think of something over the next few weeks. Who would like to begin?"

Oh, boy. I knew what I was thankful for. My trip to New York City. But I could not put that on the list yet because it would ruin my Show and Share surprise.

Lots of other kids thought of things to put on the list. They were thankful for their friends and their families. They were thankful for the autumn leaves and because they were going to have company for the holiday. I was thankful for those things, too.

When the list was finished, Ms. Colman said, "Now it is time for Show and Share."

"I am thankful for that!" I called out.

"Why don't you begin, Karen," Ms. Colman said.

This was a good idea. If I had not gone first, I think I would have burst.

"I would like to share my Thanksgiving news," I said. "I am going to New York City with my family. We are going to stay in a hotel where we can see the Macy's

Thanksgiving Day parade. We are going to the planetarium. I am going to see my pen pal, Maxie. And I am going to have the best Thanksgiving ever!''

When I finished, I sat down. I felt much better now that I had shared my Thanksgiving news.

5

The Invitation

Just before dinner on Friday night the phone rang. Seth had come home early and he answered it.

"Hi, Mom. How are you? How is Pop feeling?" he asked.

It was Granny and Grandad. I was glad Seth was home when they called. Maybe he could cheer them up. Seth talked to them while Mommy, Andrew, and I finished fixing dinner.

Before we sat down to eat, we each got to talk on the phone. When it was my turn,

I told Granny and Grandad about our Thanksgiving trip. I knew they were happy for me. But still, it sounded as though something were wrong. I asked Seth about Granny and Grandad while we ate our dinner.

"I know Grandad is better from his heart attack. But he and Granny do not sound happy lately," I said.

"You are right," said Seth. "Grandad is a lot better than he was right after his heart attack. But he is still weak. That means the farmhands have to take care of the farm. And he and Granny do not leave the house much. They are probably just plain lonely."

"Why don't we ask them to come visit us?" I said. "They would not be lonely here."

"That is a very good idea, Karen," said Mommy. "We cannot seem to cheer them up on the phone. It would be better if they were with us."

"But it is not easy to get them to leave the farm," said Seth. "Maybe if we tell them we want them to spend the holidays with us, they would agree to make the trip. They could come next week. That way they will feel right at home by Thanksgiving. They can stay here through Christmas and even New Year's Eve."

"If they want to stay longer, that would be fine, too," said Mommy. "I think this is a wonderful idea."

Seth called Granny and Grandad after dinner. They did not seem to think the idea was as wonderful as we did. We listened to Seth try to convince them to visit us.

"Yes, I know it is hard to leave your farm," he said. "I know you have been there for four decades. But you will only be visiting us for the holidays. Then you will go back. Please just think about it. We would really love to have you with us."

I hoped Granny and Grandad would call back right away to tell us they were coming. But they did not. Mommy and Seth called them a few more times on Saturday and Sunday. But still they would not say yes.

"Please just keep thinking about it," said Mommy.

Mommy passed the phone to me.

"We miss you and really want to see you!" I said.

I passed the phone to Andrew.

"We love you, Granny and Grandad," he said.

Still they did not say yes. Finally, on Monday night the phone rang. Seth answered it. He listened for a minute, then said, "That is terrific news! I will call the airlines and call you right back."

"Yippee! They are coming!" I said.

"That is right," said Seth. "And do you know what? They sound happier already. They said they are looking forward to the trip."

Seth made the airline reservations. Granny and Grandad would fly to Connecticut on Thursday. They would stay with us until sometime in January. This was good news. But one thing was worrying me.

"What about our trip to New York?" I asked.

"Granny and Grandad can come with us," replied Seth.

All right! Now I could look forward to Thursday and Thanksgiving, too.

A New Room

Creak. Groan. What was going on? It was Tuesday morning. I hurried downstairs to find out.

Mommy was in the den moving furniture around.

"Why are you doing that?" I asked.

"We need to turn the den into a guest room for Granny and Grandad," Mommy replied.

"What about the guest room upstairs?" I asked. "They stayed there the last time they visited."

"That was before Grandad got sick. He is too weak to go up and down steps now," said Mommy. "Seth is going to see about getting a second-hand sofa bed. And he will bring home a couple of tables he made. They will be perfect nightstands."

"We should decorate the room, too," I said. "Could that be my job?"

"That would be a big help," Mommy replied.

"I want to help, too," said Andrew.

He was standing behind me in his pajamas, rubbing the sleep from his eyes.

"Come on, kids," said Mommy. "We can work on the room this afternoon. Now it is time to get ready for school."

School was fun. But I was happy when it was over. I wanted to decorate for Granny and Grandad's visit. I went straight to the den when I got home. I wanted to see if it looked any different than when I left. It did.

"Where did the couch go?" I asked.

"It was picked up by the Salvation Army," said Mommy. "Seth found a sofa bed for us. It will be here tomorrow."

Andrew ran out of the kitchen waving a pink turkey on a stick.

"This is for the new room," he said.

"I like it," I replied. I really did, too. It was a funny turkey. It would cheer up Granny and Grandad.

I washed up fast and ate my snack. Then I set to work.

"Where should we put my turkey?" asked Andrew.

I looked around the room. I saw a small vase on the bookcase.

"Let's see how it looks here," I said. I put the turkey in the vase.

"Now it is a turkey-flower," said Andrew.

I ran to my room to get the paper pumpkins I had made in school. I punched a hole at the top of each one and strung them on a piece of yellow ribbon. Mommy helped me hang it across the windows.

"The turkey and pumpkins look beautiful," she said.

I wanted to show Seth what we had done. But he did not get home until a long time after dinner. By then, Mommy, Andrew, and I were cleaning up the den. Seth carried in the two tables he had made. They looked like tables you would see in a fancy store. (Seth is a very good carpenter.)

"This room looks great," said Seth.

The room looked even better the next day. When I arrived home from school on Wednesday, the sofa bed was there. It was blue with colored speckles. I helped Mommy vacuum it and put on the sheets.

That night, Seth carried in two small lamps he had borrowed from someone at his workshop. He put one on each nightstand and turned them both on.

"The room looks so cozy," I said.

"You three have done a terrific job," replied Seth. "Thank you."

Finally Thursday arrived. Seth came home early because it was a special day.

"Is everybody ready?" he said.

We took one last look at the new guest

room. Mommy had brought in a vase of fresh flowers and a bowl of fruit. The room looked perfect.

We piled into the car and buckled up. We were on our way to the airport to pick up Granny and Grandad.

A Happy Reunion

"*D*o *your ears hang low? Do they wobble to and fro? Can you tie them in a knot? Can you tie them in a bow?*"

Andrew and I were sitting in the back seat of the car singing silly songs.

"I see the first sign for the airport," said Seth. "We will be there soon."

We followed the signs and parked the car in the airport lot. When we were inside we checked a TV screen that listed the gate numbers.

"Granny and Grandad will be on Flight

thirty-eight from Omaha. Can you find it on the screen, Karen?" asked Seth.

I looked down the list but I did not see it. Maybe I had missed it. I started from the top again. Sure enough, there it was, in the middle.

"Gate Six," I said.

"Let's go," said Mommy.

We reached the gate with plenty of time to spare. Mommy and Seth took Andrew and me to the bathrooms. Then we looked in the gift shop.

Finally an announcement came over the loudspeaker. *"Flight thirty-eight from Omaha, now arriving at Gate Six."*

We hurried to Gate 6 to watch the plane come in. Andrew and I waved while it was landing, just in case Granny and Grandad were watching.

In a few minutes, a flight attendant walked into the waiting room. She was pushing a wheelchair. The person in the wheelchair was Grandad. Granny was walking next to him, holding his hand.

We ran to them and threw our arms around Grandad and Granny. I tried to put a smile on my face. But I felt sad. Grandad looked so old.

"Thank you," Seth said to the attendant. "We can take it from here."

"Are you okay, Grandad?" I asked. "Did something bad happen on the plane?"

"I am fine," Grandad replied. "I was just feeling a little tired from the trip. Granny thought the wheelchair would be a good idea in the airport."

"We are happy you are here," said Mommy.

"Extra happy," said Andrew.

"Come on," said Seth. "Let's go pick up your luggage."

We went straight to the baggage pickup area. All kinds of bags were going round and round on the conveyor belt.

"Just call out when you see one of yours," said Seth.

"There's one!" called Grandad.

"There's another!" called Granny.

ARRIVALS

Granny and Grandad were staying a long time, so they needed lots of things. We piled seven bags onto a cart. Seth pushed the cart through the airport. Mommy helped Grandad.

We did not talk much on the ride home. Mommy said Granny and Grandad needed to rest.

As soon as we walked through the door of the little house, we showed Granny and Grandad their new room.

"Ta-daa!" I said.

"This is beautiful," said Granny.

"The couch opens up into a comfortable bed," said Mommy. "Come. I have a snack ready for us in the kitchen. You must be hungry after your trip."

We sat in the kitchen and ate and talked.

"I am happy you will be with us on Thanksgiving," I said. "We will have fun in New York!"

"The trip sounds wonderful," said Granny. "But I really think it would be too much for Grandad and me. We will manage just fine in Stoneybrook on our own."

This was not good news. I would be sad if Granny and Grandad did not come to New York with us. I hoped we would be able to change their minds.

8

Horn of Plenty

As soon as I woke up the next morning, I ran to Granny's and Grandad's room. Andrew was right behind me.

"How did you sleep?" I asked. "Was your bed comfortable? Did any noises wake you up?"

"We had a very restful night," said Granny.

"You did not tell us about Sheppy last night," said Andrew.

(Sheppy is Granny's and Grandad's dog.)

"Sheppy is just fine," said Grandad. "So is Pearl."

(Pearl is their cat.)

We visited with Granny and Grandad until Mommy sent us upstairs to get dressed. I did not want to leave. I wanted to stay with Granny and Grandad all day. But I knew I would not be allowed to miss school.

When I was dressed, I found a bowl of Krispy Krunchy cereal waiting at my place. I wished Grandad's pancakes were there. Grandad used to love to cook. But I guess he was too tired to cook much these days.

Beep, beep. We were finishing breakfast when Andrew's carpool came to take him to preschool. That meant my school bus would be arriving any minute. We grabbed our jackets and kissed everyone good-bye.

"See you later," I said.

Granny and Grandad watched us from the window. I waved to them as I ran to the bus stop. It was so much fun having them at our house.

School was fun, too. In the morning, we collected fall leaves in the courtyard outside our room. We found maple, oak, and sycamore leaves. We made them into a collage and hung it on the bulletin board.

"Is it okay if I bring some more leaves home for Granny and Grandad?" I asked. "They are staying at my house."

"Of course," Ms. Colman replied.

After lunch, we were given an important assignment.

"I would like you to make Thanksgiving decorations to brighten up Stoneybrook Manor," said Ms. Colman.

Hooray! I love making decorations. And it is nice to cheer up the people at Stoneybrook Manor. That is where some senior citizens live.

Ms. Colman set out construction paper, yarn, crayons, markers, scissors, and glue.

"You may make anything that reminds you of fall and Thanksgiving," Ms. Colman said. "You may make pumpkins, turkeys, pilgrims, cornucopias."

I waved my hand and Ms. Colman called on me.

"What is a cornucopia?" I asked.

"A cornucopia is a basket shaped like a horn. It is filled with fruit, flowers, and vegetables. It is also called a horn of plenty. It is a symbol of good times," Ms. Colman explained.

"I am having a very good time today, so I will make one of those," I said.

We were allowed to sit anywhere while we worked. I sat with Hannie and Nancy at the back of the room. Nancy was making a chain of paper doll pilgrims. Hannie was making a snowflake mobile. While we worked, we talked.

Nancy was excited about her plans for Thanksgiving. She had just found out that she was going to Massachusetts with her parents and her baby brother, Danny.

"My parents' friends have five children," said Nancy. "That means there will be eleven of us for Thanksgiving dinner. We will all cook something. It will be a feast!"

I told my friends that Granny and Grandad might not come to New York. "I hope they will change their minds," I said.

I sat back and looked at the work I had done so far on my cornucopia. I had used yellow construction paper to make the horn. I was filling it with paper fruit and flowers.

I was having a happy day. And I was making a beautiful horn of plenty.

9

A Walk With Grandad

After school, I jumped off the bus, waved good-bye to Nancy, and ran home. I opened the door and found Grandad sitting by himself in the living room. He looked sad.

"Hi, Grandad. Where is everyone?" I asked.

"Seth is at work. Your mother, brother, and Granny went downtown," Grandad replied.

"That leaves just you and me then. I will make us an afterschool snack," I said.

I made peanut butter and jelly on crackers. Grandad seemed to like his snack. I wanted to cheer him up. So while we were eating I told him everything I did in school. I told him about my cornucopia, and about Stoneybrook Manor. I told him about Ms. Colman, about my friends, and my classmates.

"I almost forgot! I brought you something," I said.

I found the leaves I had collected.

"Do you know what kinds they are?" I asked.

"Let me see," said Grandad. "This one is a sycamore leaf. This is a maple leaf. And this is an oak leaf."

"You are right! You get an A plus," I said.

Grandad smiled. I could tell he was starting to feel better. Maybe he had just been lonely. I wanted to go outside. But I did not want to leave him alone again.

"Do you want to take a walk with me, Grandad? Just a little walk?" I asked.

"All right," replied Grandad. "A little

walk will be nice. I will get my sweater."

We had walked together in my neighborhood before. But there was something new I wanted to show him. We went a few blocks to the construction site where my friends and I had painted a panel on a big fence. It was a cartoon of *The Space Game*. (*The Space Game* was a very exciting movie.)

"We won first prize for the funniest panel," I said.

"It is wonderful!" exclaimed Grandad. "You deserved that prize."

I did not want to keep Grandad out too long. So we headed back to the house. On the way, we met Kathryn and Willie Barnes. (Kathryn is six; Willie is five.) They had met Grandad before. But I introduced them again.

Then we met Bobby and Alicia. (Bobby is my classmate. Alicia is his little sister. She is Andrew's age.) I reintroduced them to Grandad, too.

Before we returned to the little house, I took Grandad next door to say hello to

Nancy. I knocked on the door. Mrs. Dawes opened it carrying Danny in her arms. Then Nancy ran downstairs. She was carrying her kitten, Pokey.

We stood at the door and talked a few minutes. Then it was time for Grandad and me to go home.

"Thank you for stopping by," said Mrs. Dawes. "I hope you enjoy your visit."

That night at dinner, Grandad told everyone about our afternoon. He sounded very happy.

"I had a delicious peanut butter and jelly snack. I saw a prizewinning panel. And I got to say hello to Karen's friends. We had a lot of fun," said Grandad.

"Speaking of fun, have you given any thought to the Thanksgiving trip?" asked Seth.

"We are thinking that if you cannot go, we might skip it this year," said Mommy.

Omigosh! Skip our trip? That would be *awful*. I was *dying* to see the parade.

"But, Mommy, we were going to be way

up high with the balloons," I said. "We have to go."

"Of course you do," said Granny. "Do not even think about canceling the trip."

"We will be fine here," said Grandad. "Especially now that I know the neighborhood so well."

Grandad winked at me. Thank goodness. We were going to take our trip after all.

School Visitors

It was Monday. Another Show and Share day. I knew just what I wanted to share, too.

I was so excited about our trip to New York that over the weekend I did something special. I made a gigundoly beautiful diorama of the parade. I filled a very large box with paper balloons, buildings, and people. I made the balloons in the shapes of my favorite characters. I made the people waving and smiling.

"I do not see how that will fit on the

school bus with you," said Mommy. "It is much too big."

We had just finished breakfast. Andrew's carpool had picked him up. My school bus would be arriving any minute.

"I have to take it with me," I said. "I already showed it to Nancy. Now I want Hannie to see it. And Ms. Colman. I want everyone in my class to see it."

"I am sorry, Karen," replied Mommy. "I cannot drive you to school. Seth has been working hard lately and I promised to give him a hand at the workshop. He is waiting in the car for me now."

I looked at Granny and Grandad. Maybe. Just maybe.

"Could *you* take me?" I asked.

"Of course we could," said Granny. "We would be happy to."

"Are you sure?" asked Mommy.

"It will be fun," Grandad replied. "We are ready whenever you are, Karen."

Yippee! Mommy carried my diorama outside and put it in her car.

"Thank you, Mommy! See you later," I called. I waved good-bye as she and Seth drove off.

"Do you know the way?" asked Grandad.

"Of course," I replied.

I told them exactly how to go to school. Right turn. Left. Straight. Right. Park in the lot. No problem!

The three of us carried the diorama into my classroom together. It was not heavy. Just big. We put it down on the floor at the front of the room.

I was so excited about having Granny and Grandad in my classroom. I wanted to show them everything.

First I showed them where I sit. Natalie and Ricky were already at their desks, so I introduced them to my friends. (I did not tell them that Ricky is my husband. I was not sure they would approve of my being married so young, even if it is only pretend.)

Then Hannie arrived. She had met

Granny and Grandad a couple of times. She was happy to see them.

I introduced them to Hootie, our guinea pig.

"Isn't he cute?" I said.

"It is nice to have a pet at school," said Grandad. "You can learn a lot by watching and caring for an animal."

Then Ms. Colman walked in.

"Ms. Colman! Ms. Colman! This is my granny and my grandad," I said.

"I am very happy to meet you," Ms. Colman replied.

I introduced Granny and Grandad to all my classmates. I showed them our beautiful fall leaf collage. I showed them the things we had made for Stoneybrook Manor. (We had not brought our decorations over there yet.)

Then it was time for Granny and Grandad to leave. I was sorry to see them go. I could tell they liked being in my classroom. And I liked having them there.

"This has been a real treat, Karen," said

51

Grandad. "Have a good day at school."

Thanks to Granny and Grandad, I was going to have an excellent day at school. Thanks to them, my class was going to see my diorama at Show and Share.

11

A Talk With Granny

When I returned from school the next day, Granny and Grandad were waiting for me. Mommy had taken Andrew to the dentist for a checkup.

"How was school today?" asked Granny.

"It was great!" I replied. "Ms. Colman liked my New York City diorama so much that she made a special place for it on the window ledge. Nobody else has an important display like mine."

"It is not nice to brag, Karen," said Grandad.

Humph. I did not see why. A little bragging does not hurt anybody.

"What else did you do at school?" asked Granny.

"We read a cool book about a class that takes a magic school bus ride back to the time of the dinosaurs. The kids are afraid the dinosaurs are after them. They have to run away really fast."

I started running around the living room to escape from the make-believe dinosaurs that were after me.

"Eek!" I shouted.

"Karen! Karen! Please stop shouting and running in the house. I am getting a headache. And you could very easily break something," said Grandad.

Well, for heaven's sake. Grandad was grouchy. Everyone knows I shout when I am excited. Ms. Colman has to remind me to use my indoor voice all the time. But she says it nicely. And I never break anything when I run around. Well, hardly ever.

I did not like being scolded by Grandad.

"I guess I better do my homework," I said.

I ran to my room and sat on my bed with Goosie. I had wanted to tell Granny and Grandad more things about my day. I wanted to tell them I got all my spelling words right. And when we played dodge ball, Mrs. Mackey, the gym teacher, said I run as fast as the wind.

But I was better off telling Goosie. Grandad would just say I was bragging. And if I showed him how fast I ran, he would say I might break something. I felt as though I could not do anything right. I started to cry a little.

Knock, knock. It was Granny.

"May I come in?" she asked.

I nodded. Granny sat on my bed and put her arm around me.

"Why are you crying?" she asked.

"I do not like it when Grandad scolds me," I said. "I do not want him to be angry with me."

"He is not angry at you," said Granny.

"He is sad. He misses the farm. He feels bad that he cannot do the things he was once able to do. And today he just does not feel well. That is why he is acting cranky. He loves you very much. Do you understand that?"

"I guess so," I replied.

I know that sometimes when I am not feeling well, I snap at my friends. But it does not mean I do not like them anymore.

"Why don't you wash up and come have a snack?" said Granny. "You must be hungry."

I washed up and went downstairs. Grandad was sitting at the kitchen table. A plate of crackers, cheese, and sliced apples was waiting for me. There was a cup filled with grape juice, too.

I told Grandad about my spelling test. I told him how I won dodge ball because I ran so fast. I told him quietly and I did not brag. I wanted Grandad to feel better. And you know what? I think he did.

"How about telling me some more about

those dinosaurs?" said Grandad.

"Okay," I replied. "I will even draw you pictures of them. They are big and scaly."

I went upstairs to get paper and markers. It was going to be a nice afternoon with Grandad after all.

12

Helping Out

"Look how clean my teeth are," said Andrew. He smiled a big, funny smile so I could see all his teeth. "And I got a brand-new toothbrush."

"I know. You told me already," I said.

Andrew and I were helping Mommy and Granny make dinner. Grandad was resting. Seth was at work.

Seth was still at work when we ate our dinner. He was still at work when it was almost time for bed. I was in my pajamas and brushing my teeth when I heard him come in. I spit out the toothpaste and ran downstairs.

"Hi!" I said. "We missed you at dinner. We made excellent meatballs and spaghetti."

"I am sorry I missed meatballs and spaghetti. And I am even sorrier I missed being with you," Seth replied. "I know I have been working very long hours these days."

"How is it going at the shop?" asked Grandad.

"Not so well. I work and I work. But the way it is going, I will never have all my holiday orders ready on time," Seth replied.

"Something has to be done," said Mommy. "You need more help at the workshop."

"You are right," replied Seth. "But I do not have the money to hire someone right now."

"I could stay home from school and help!" I said.

"Me, too!" said Andrew.

"Thank you, kids. But school is too important to miss," Seth replied.

"I was thinking that I could help you more," said Mommy. "I helped out for awhile when Ruth went to Canada to take care of her mother. Remember how well that worked out?"

(Ruth is the woman who runs Seth's office.)

"You will not have to hire a baby-sitter this time, either," said Granny. "Grandad and I are here. We would be happy to help out, too."

"We would be more than happy. We would love it," said Grandad.

The grown-ups started talking all at once. They seemed to have a lot to figure out. Finally Seth said, "Okay, then. We are all set."

"What is all set?" I asked. They had been

talking so fast, I could not follow them.

They took turns explaining the new arrangement. Mommy was going to help Seth full-time in his shop until Christmas.

"That way Seth can work more regular hours," said Mommy.

Granny was going to run the house.

"I can cook, clean, and drive to the stores," said Granny.

Grandad was going to be in charge of Andrew and me whenever we were not in school.

"You may have to play a little more quietly than usual. But I promise we will have fun," said Grandad.

"I know lots of quiet things we can do," I said. "We can read books together. We can make holiday decorations and cards. We can watch videos."

"I want to watch Winnie-the-Pooh," said Andrew. "I like Pooh and Piglet."

"This is terrific," said Seth. "Thank you, everyone."

"It is time for bed now," said Mommy.

"We will come upstairs in a minute to say good night. Our new arrangement will start first thing tomorrow."

I went to bed thinking about our new plan. I decided I was going to like it just fine.

We will come and see in a minute to how agreed the One man, dog to agree we'll said
bed there, found and for a most he we had
it wait to best the of us of him been
park a parked we'll park in a Now and
ma

The New Baby-sitter

Wednesday was the first day of our new arrangement. It went just fine. By Thursday I felt as though our family had been doing things this way forever.

Granny was out shopping for dinner when Andrew and I returned from school. Grandad was waiting for us with a snack. It was a plate of corn chips with cheese on top. I reached for a chip.

"Wait," said Grandad. "It gets even better."

As soon as we washed up, Grandad popped the chips into the microwave. The cheese melted and bubbled. When we ate our snack, the chips were crunchy and the cheese was warm and stringy. We had homemade lemonade to drink.

"Yum. This is the best snack ever," I said.

"And it was easy," replied Grandad. "I could make it while I was sitting down."

"Let's make some more," I said. "Then Mommy, Seth, and Granny can have a snack when they come home."

"Good idea," said Grandad.

The snack really was easy to make. It did not take very long.

"Now what should we do?" I asked.

I did not have any homework. And it was raining outside, so Andrew and I could not go outside to play with our friends.

"I want to play tag," said Andrew.

"I do not think that is such a good

idea," said Grandad. He looked worried.

I decided to help out. "That game is too wild," I said. "We could knock something over."

Grandad looked relieved.

"Let's have a marching band. I will be the leader," said Andrew.

Grandad looked worried again.

"A band is too noisy," I said. "Grandad could get a headache."

"I have an idea," said Grandad. "Who would like to go on a peanut hunt?"

"Me!" said Andrew.

"Me, too. But I do not think we have any peanuts," I said.

"No problem," said Grandad. "We can draw some."

We found paper and markers and drew peanuts. They were pretty silly. We made them all different colors and put funny faces on them.

"You two go upstairs, while I hide the peanuts," said Grandad.

A few minutes later, he made believe he was blowing a trumpet.

"Toot-toot-toot! The peanut hunt is about to begin!" he called.

Andrew and I ran downstairs to look for paper peanuts. Whenever we got close to one, Grandad told us we were getting warmer. If we walked away, he told us we were getting colder. This was a very good game to play. We were having fun without running or making noise. And Grandad got to sit while we played.

"Karen, you are warm," said Grandad.

I took another step.

"Warmer," he said.

I kept taking steps in the same direction.

"Warmer. Warmer. Hot. Hot. Hot!" said Grandad.

"I found a peanut!" I said.

Then Andrew found one. Then I found another. Soon we had found all the peanuts. Grandad gave us a penny for each one. Then he taught us a silly peanut song.

"Oh, a peanut sat on a railroad track. His heart was all a-flutter. Along came the five-fifteen. Uh-oh, peanut butter!"

Grandad was laughing. He was not cranky or sad. He was happy. And so were we.

14

A Change of Plans

Every day Andrew and I spent with Grandad was fun.

Granny helped baby-sit sometimes. But mostly she was too busy running errands and taking care of the house.

Mommy went to work with Seth. They even worked on Saturday and Sunday. Now that Mommy was helping at the work-shop, Seth could come home for dinner. He was about a hundred times happier. We all were.

"This dinner is delicious," said Seth.

"It sure is, Granny," I said. "More lasagna, please."

It was Monday night. We were eating vegetable lasagna and salad. Andrew and I had helped Granny make the salad.

"When will it be Thanksgiving?" asked Andrew. "My teacher told us, but I forgot."

"Thanksgiving is on Thursday," Mommy replied. "That is only three days away."

Seth turned to Granny and Grandad.

"How do you feel about staying in Stoneybrook?" he asked. "Are you sure that is what you want to do? If not, we will make a reservation for you in New York."

"Thank you, but we still think it best if we stay here," said Granny.

"What will you *do* for Thanksgiving?" asked Mommy. "You have been working so hard helping us out. We want you to do something nice."

"Oh, we will," said Grandad. "Granny

promised to make me a turkey with all the fixings, didn't you?"

"I certainly did," said Granny.

"But who will eat it with you?" I asked.

Grandad looked around the room. "Why, Midgie and Rocky can each have a taste. If they behave themselves, that is," he replied.

"What else will you do?" asked Mommy.

"Maybe Grandad will take me to the movies," said Granny. "Or we can rent one. We will read. And we enjoy playing checkers."

"We might even have a peanut hunt," said Grandad.

I could tell he was trying to be cheerful. But I was starting to feel bad about Granny's and Grandad's staying home alone. Their plans did not sound very exciting. On Thanksgiving it is nice to be with lots of people.

"Will you excuse us for a minute?" said

Seth. "Lisa, will you help me in the living room?"

Mommy and Seth went to the other room. I could hear them whispering. Then they came back.

"Kids, we know that you were looking forward to our trip to New York. We know that it would be a lot of fun. But we think that staying home will be fun, too," said Seth.

"If we stay here, the six of us can have a lovely Thanksgiving meal together," said Mommy.

"Oh, no," said Grandad. "You must not cancel your plans. We told you we will be fine."

"We know you will be fine. But we will not be. We do not think we could enjoy our trip if we leave you behind," said Seth. "But we know we will have a good time if we are here together."

"But . . . but," I said.

I did not finish my sentence, though.

Even Andrew knew enough to keep quiet. Granny and Grandad looked so pleased. We did not want them to feel bad.

"If you are really going to stay, I will buy a great big turkey tomorrow," said Granny.

"We are staying in Stoneybrook," said Mommy. "And that is final."

Shopping

On Tuesday, Granny invited me to go to the supermarket with her to buy our turkey.

"How big is our turkey going to be?" I asked. I was pushing our shopping cart into the store.

"There will be six of us. So our turkey should be at least six pounds," Granny replied.

"Will there be enough for Midgie and Rocky? Will there be enough for leftovers? I love leftovers," I said.

"We better get a seven-pound turkey just to be safe," Granny replied.

On the way to the meat section we passed the fruits and vegetables.

"We need cranberries for cranberry sauce. And we should get sweet potatoes, too," said Granny.

"The potatoes are over here," I said.

I led Granny to the potato bin. Only three potatoes were left. They looked pretty banged up.

"Oh, my. Thanksgiving is only a day and a half away. There is not much left to buy," said Granny. "Let's see if we can find those cranberries."

The cranberries were completely sold out. Boo.

"We better hurry and get our turkey," I said. "We do not want anyone else to buy the last one."

I raced to the meat department. Granny had to run to keep up with me. There was not a single turkey in sight.

We looked everywhere. Finally Granny

found two tiny ones buried under some packages of chicken wings.

"We cannot buy these turkeys. They do not look fresh at all," said Granny.

"Then what will we eat?" I asked.

"The chicken wings look nice," said Granny. "And there are plenty of them."

"But I like turkey and stuffing on Thanksgiving," I said.

Granny thought for a minute. Then she said, "This is what we will do. We will bake the chicken wings. We will arrange them in the shape of a turkey. We will put our stuffing in the center."

"Cool!" I said. "We will have a chicken turkey. No one else in Stoneybrook will have one of those. No one else in the whole world will have one."

We bought every chicken wing in the store. Then we walked up and down the aisles looking for Thanksgiving things to eat. Here is what we ended up with: canned cranberry sauce, canned lima beans, canned sweet potatoes, a box of stuffing mix, two frozen pumpkin pies, a roll of chocolate chip cookie batter, and a turkey-shaped cookie cutter. (I wanted a chocolate turkey, but they were all gone. Chocolate chip turkey-shaped cookies were the next best thing.)

"We did very well considering what was left," said Granny.

When we got home the telephone was ringing. It was Nancy. She did not sound happy.

"Our Thanksgiving dinner was canceled," she said. "We are not going to Massachusetts after all. We will not get to see our friends. And we have nothing to eat but the cranberry sauce and the two vegetables we made."

"I am sorry about your plans," I said. "We are not having turkey either. The good ones were all gone."

When Mommy and Seth came home, I told them about Nancy's plans. Mommy and Seth told Granny and Grandad. The grown-ups started talking all at once just the way they had before. When they finished, Mommy called Mrs. Dawes.

"I heard your plans were canceled," she said. "You are welcome to join us if you do not mind having chicken wings on Thanksgiving."

I crossed my fingers and hoped Mrs. Dawes would say they did not mind. Guess what. She did! It looked as if Thanksgiving might turn out better than we thought.

16

Karen's Idea

On Wednesday I got to have a chocolate turkey after all. Ms. Colman gave each kid in the class a turkey wrapped in gold foil.

"Happy Thanksgiving, everyone," she said.

I told you Ms. Colman is nice.

School let out early because of the holiday. It was a sunny day. At home, Andrew and I ate a snack. Then we went outside to play with the kids in the neighborhood.

I thought about something. I had just realized that if we had still been going on our trip to New York, we would probably be leaving that very minute. And tomorrow morning we would have been watching the Macy's Thanksgiving Day parade.

I was looking forward to our big Thanksgiving dinner at home. But I was sad we were not going to see the parade. We could watch it on TV. But a TV parade is not the same as a real, live parade. Then I got an idea.

"Hey, everyone!" I cried. My friends gathered around me. "Tomorrow is Thanksgiving and none of us are going to the Macy's parade," I said. "I think we should have our own Thanksgiving Day parade right here. All in favor raise your hands and say, 'Turkey.' "

"Turkey!" my friends replied.

Seven hands flew up in the air. They belonged to Andrew, me, Nancy, Bobby, Alicia, Kathryn, and Willie. I was sorry the Barton kids were not around. They are the new kids on the block. There are five of them. They were spending the holiday with friends from their old neighborhood.

"I want to get dressed up for the parade," said Alicia. "I want to be a Thanksgiving princess."

"I have party hats at home," said Nancy. "I can bring them for everyone."

"Great," I replied. "Balloons are important, too. Does anyone have twenty-foot-tall Disney balloons with helium in them?"

No one did. Some kids had leftover birthday balloons. Bobby had balloons from Halloween with "Boo!" written on them.

"If we attach them to long sticks, they will look like they are flying in the air," said Kathryn.

"We need to have floats, too," I said.

"I can bring my red wagon," said Willie.

"And Midgie could ride in it," said Andrew. "We could even make her a pilgrim hat."

Everyone had good ideas. I had one more important question to ask.

"Who should be the leader of the parade? I think it should be the person who thought of the parade in the first place," I said. "All in favor raise your hand and say, 'Karen.' "

The hands did not go up very high. And no one said my name very loudly. But nobody said I could not be the leader. So that meant I could be.

17

Thanksgiving Morning

"Gobble, gobble, gobble," said Andrew. "Wake up, Karen. It is Thanksgiving!"

It was Thursday morning. Andrew was standing at the door to my room. I am usually the first one out of bed. But I had stayed up late the night before. I was thinking about our parade and trying to write a Thanksgiving poem.

"Happy Thanksgiving, Andrew," I said.

I could hear pots and pans clanging in the kitchen. I jumped up, got dressed, and ran downstairs. I did not want to miss anything important.

Grandad was resting in his room. I gave him a Thanksgiving hug. Then I asked him a Thanksgiving riddle.

"What is smarter than a talking turkey?" I said.

"I give up," replied Grandad.

"A spelling bee!" I said.

Grandad thought this was very funny. I left him laughing and went into the kitchen. Mommy, Seth, and Granny were already cleaning and cooking.

"How about having your breakfast and then helping me make some soup?" said Granny. "I found a package of vegetable soup mix in the cupboard."

I ate my Krispy Krunchy cereal very fast. Then I helped Granny measure and mix.

When I finished, Mommy said, "Would you like to help me baste the chicken wings?"

"Sure," I replied. I brushed barbecue sauce over each of the chicken wings.

Meanwhile, Andrew was helping Seth set the table.

"Do you know how many places we need to set?" asked Seth.

I counted in my head. There were six of us and four in Nancy's family. That made ten places. I whispered the answer to Mommy and Granny, but I did not say it out loud. It took Andrew a long time to count on his fingers, but finally he called out, "Ten!"

"Good for you," replied Seth.

"Mommy, when is the Macy's parade? I want to watch it on TV," I said.

Mommy looked at her watch.

"It starts in about an hour," she replied. "Why don't you call Nancy and invite her to watch it with you?"

"All right," I replied.

I called Nancy. She promised to come over as soon as she could. I decided it would be fun to make decorations and placecards while we watched the parade. I ran upstairs and found paper, glue, streamers, markers, and glitter. Before I knew it, Nancy was at the door and the parade was starting. Nancy, Andrew, and I sat down to watch together.

"I see Winnie-the-Pooh," said Andrew. "Hi, Pooh!"

"Here come the Flintstones," I said. Nancy and I sang the Flintstones song.

We named every one of the balloons. When we were not jumping up and down and pointing to things in the parade, we were busy making decorations and place-cards. By the time the parade was over, we had everything we needed.

Our placecards were shaped like turkeys. On each one was written a guest's name. We put a card at every seat. We filled three vases with paper flowers. Then Seth helped us hang streamers around the room.

"You have done a beautiful job," said Granny.

"Thank you," Nancy and I replied.

Our work inside the house was done. It was time to get ready for our parade.

"Midgie! Midgie, come!" I called.

"I just saw her go the other way," said Andrew.

"Do not be shy, Midgie. You will look very nice in a pilgrim's hat," I said.

I do not think she believed me.

18

The Parade

Clang! Clang! Clang! Bangity! Bang! Bang!
Andrew was using two pot lids to make cymbals. Bobby and Alicia were using pots and wooden spoons to make drums.

"Ladies and gentlemen! Children of all ages!" I called. "The very first Stoneybrook Thanksgiving Day Parade is about to begin."

(I could not remember how a parade starts. So I started ours like a circus.)

Clang! Clang! Clang! Bangity! Bang! Bang!
In New York City, the streets are lined

with people whenever there is a parade. So we rounded up as many relatives, guests, and neighbors as we could. We wanted them to cheer for us as we marched up and down the street.

Here is what I wore to lead the parade: red tights, blue shorts, white T-shirt, jean jacket, and a pair of Granny's white gloves. I put one of Nancy's party hats on my head. And I draped a banner over my shoulder. It said *Happy Thanksgiving* inside a beautiful glitter border. I was carrying a baton. (It was really a folding umbrella with streamers on it.)

My friends were dressed up, too. They were princesses, pilgrims, and movie stars.

Midgie's pilgrim hat was hanging under her chin because she kept knocking it off with her paw. And she walked next to Willy's wagon instead of riding in it. But that was okay. Her tail was wagging and she was smiling. So I knew she was having fun.

We were carrying balloons and cutouts of Disney characters on sticks. We held them high in the air as we marched up and down our street.

Clang! Clang! Bangity! Bang!

"Hi, everyone!" I called as we passed the little house.

My family and Nancy's were standing together. Even Grandad was outside. He was sitting in a chair on the lawn.

We marched and waved, and even did a line dance. Seth was taking pictures. And Bobby's father was videotaping us. He promised to make a copy of the tape for anyone who wanted one.

Andrew and I wanted a tape. We wanted to show the parade to our big-house family when we were at Daddy's in December.

I put my arm around Andrew and waved and smiled into the camera. Watching the Macy's parade in person would have been fun. But being in our own parade was exciting, too.

When the parade was over, Mommy asked us to come inside. It was time for our Thanksgiving dinner.

19

Thanksgiving Dinner

"Pass the chicken wings, please," I said.

The plate was at the other end of the table. It was passed from Mommy to Seth to Mrs. Dawes to Granny to Mr. Dawes to Nancy to me.

"Thank you," I said.

We had already eaten the soup Granny and I had made. It turned out very well. Now we were eating the main course. The chicken wings were not in the shape of a turkey anymore. But they had looked very nice when we started. I had spelled out the word turkey using lima beans at the bottom of the serving plate. Seth took a picture of it.

"This is one turkey we will not want to forget," he said.

I served myself a few chicken wings and some stuffing. I already had sweet potatoes, lima beans, and the cranberry sauce the Daweses had brought on my plate. Everything tasted very good. I think that is because we were laughing and talking so much. Having a good time makes everything more tasty.

Midgie and Rocky were having fun, too. Danny was throwing his food in the air. Midgie and Rocky were catching it.

Clink, clink. Grandad tapped on his glass with a spoon.

"I would like to say a few words," he said.

Everyone stopped talking and turned to Grandad.

"At first I did not want to leave Nebraska to come here for Thanksgiving. You see,

Nebraska is a place I love. But now I am with the family I love. I am with the family who canceled an exciting trip so we could celebrate the holiday together. We are joined by wonderful friends. And we are eating a very funny dinner. I have much to be grateful for this Thanksgiving. So happy holiday and thank you all."

We raised our glasses to Grandad.

"Happy Thanksgiving," we said.

Clink, clink. I tapped my glass with my spoon. Everyone turned to look at me. They looked surprised.

"I wrote a Thanksgiving poem last night," I said. "I would like to read it to you." I stood up and read my poem loudly enough for everyone to hear.

"We were going to New York City.
But now I'm glad we stayed.
We had family and friends to dinner.
And a special Thanksgiving parade!"

I sat down.

"Karen, that poem is wonderful!" said Mommy.

"Bravo!" said Seth.

It was time for dessert. We set out a plate of chocolate chip turkey cookies. Then we popped our frozen pumpkin pies into the microwave. When the pies were ready, we served them with fresh whipped cream.

It could not have been as good as home-made dessert. But it must have been all right. Because by the time dinner was over, not one cookie or pie crumb was left.

20

A Cozy Night

After dinner, Nancy, Andrew, and I played in my room. The grown-ups visited downstairs. Then Danny started to cry. He cried and cried and would not stop. So the Daweses decided to go home.

Granny and Grandad rested in their room while Andrew and I helped Mommy and Seth clean up the kitchen. We were just about finished when the doorbell rang. It was Bobby.

"Hi," he said. "My dad made a copy of

the parade tape and asked me to bring it over."

"Cool!" I said.

"Please thank your dad for us," said Seth.

By then Granny and Grandad had woken up, so we watched the parade tape together.

It started with me saying, "Ladies and gentlemen! Children of all ages!"

"I want to rewind the tape. I want to watch that again," I said.

"We will never see the rest if we start rewinding now. You can watch it as much as you want tomorrow," said Mommy.

I was glad we watched the rest of the tape. I had been so busy leading the parade that I had not seen everything that was happening. I had not seen Midgie leave the parade to chase a squirrel up a tree. I had not seen Alicia trip over her princess costume. (She did not hurt herself.) And I had not seen Bobby's spoon fall down the sewer. (He had to use a stick to bang on his pot after that.) Funny things had been going on all the time.

When the video was over, Andrew said, "I am hungry."

"Me, too," I said.

"Me three," said Seth.

"I guess it is time to eat again," said Mommy.

We spread the leftovers out on the table. We were allowed to take whatever we wanted. That is my favorite kind of meal.

We took turns piling food on our plates, then returned to the TV room. We were in time to see the end of a football game. Then one of my favorite movies, *Miracle on 34th Street*, came on. Yea! As soon as that movie comes on TV, I know Christmas is on its way.

Andrew and I were going to be at the big house for Christmas. The big house has lots of people even without any guests. I knew we would have fun there. We always do.

Finally I had to stop eating leftovers. I was starting to feel like a stuffed turkey. I

helped put the food away, then snuggled up on the couch between Granny and Grandad. Andrew was on the floor resting his head on Midgie. (They were both sleeping.) Mommy and Seth pulled their chairs close together and held hands.

When the commercials came on TV, Seth used the remote control to turn off the sound. (We do not like to watch commercials.) While we waited for the movie to come back on, I tried to decide which part of Thanksgiving I had liked the best. The parade. Our big dinner with the Daweses. Or being cozy together the way we were now. I decided I liked the whole day from start to finish.

When the movie started again, a little girl climbed onto Santa's lap. Santa had twinkling eyes and white hair.

"I like this Santa," I said to Grandad. "He reminds me of you."

"But I am luckier than he is," said Grandad.

"Why?" I asked.

"Because I have *you* for my granddaughter," Grandad replied.

Grandad seemed happy. He smiled and hugged me. I hugged him back. I was happy, too.

About the Author

ANN M. MARTIN lives in New York City and loves animals, especially cats. She has two cats of her own, Mouse and Rosie.

Other books by Ann M. Martin that you might enjoy are *Stage Fright; Me and Katie (the Pest)*; and the books in *The Baby-sitters Club* series.

Ann likes ice cream and *I Love Lucy*. And she has her own little sister, whose name is Jane.

Little Sister

Don't miss #68

KAREN'S ANGEL

"Well, we usually have a star at the top of the Christmas tree," said Elizabeth. "But our star is so old it is falling apart. We thought it would be nice to have an angel on the tree this year. Your job is to find one."

"Wow! I know everything about angels," I replied.

"My teacher says I am an angel sometimes," said Andrew.

"Your teacher is right," said Charlie. "But I think you are too heavy to sit on top of the tree."

While everyone was laughing at Charlie's joke, I was thinking. Thinking about our job finding the angel. It really *was* an important job.

LITTLE 🍎 APPLE®

Little Sister™
by Ann M. Martin, author of *The Baby-sitters Club®*

❑ MQ44300-3	#1	Karen's Witch	$2.95
❑ MQ44259-7	#2	Karen's Roller Skates	$2.95
❑ MQ44299-7	#3	Karen's Worst Day	$2.95
❑ MQ44264-3	#4	Karen's Kittycat Club	$2.95
❑ MQ44258-9	#5	Karen's School Picture	$2.95
❑ MQ44298-8	#6	Karen's Little Sister	$2.95
❑ MQ44257-0	#7	Karen's Birthday	$2.95
❑ MQ42670-2	#8	Karen's Haircut	$2.95
❑ MQ43652-X	#9	Karen's Sleepover	$2.95
❑ MQ43651-1	#10	Karen's Grandmothers	$2.95
❑ MQ43650-3	#11	Karen's Prize	$2.95
❑ MQ43649-X	#12	Karen's Ghost	$2.95
❑ MQ43648-1	#13	Karen's Surprise	$2.95
❑ MQ43646-5	#14	Karen's New Year	$2.95
❑ MQ43645-7	#15	Karen's in Love	$2.95
❑ MQ43644-9	#16	Karen's Goldfish	$2.95
❑ MQ43643-0	#17	Karen's Brothers	$2.95
❑ MQ43642-2	#18	Karen's Home Run	$2.95
❑ MQ43641-4	#19	Karen's Good-Bye	$2.95
❑ MQ44823-4	#20	Karen's Carnival	$2.95
❑ MQ44824-2	#21	Karen's New Teacher	$2.95
❑ MQ44833-1	#22	Karen's Little Witch	$2.95
❑ MQ44832-3	#23	Karen's Doll	$2.95
❑ MQ44859-5	#24	Karen's School Trip	$2.95
❑ MQ44831-5	#25	Karen's Pen Pal	$2.95
❑ MQ44830-7	#26	Karen's Ducklings	$2.75
❑ MQ44829-3	#27	Karen's Big Joke	$2.95
❑ MQ44828-5	#28	Karen's Tea Party	$2.95
❑ MQ44825-0	#29	Karen's Cartwheel	$2.75
❑ MQ45645-8	#30	Karen's Kittens	$2.95
❑ MQ45646-6	#31	Karen's Bully	$2.95
❑ MQ45647-4	#32	Karen's Pumpkin Patch	$2.95
❑ MQ45648-2	#33	Karen's Secret	$2.95
❑ MQ45650-4	#34	Karen's Snow Day	$2.95
❑ MQ45652-0	#35	Karen's Doll Hospital	$2.95
❑ MQ45651-2	#36	Karen's New Friend	$2.95
❑ MQ45653-9	#37	Karen's Tuba	$2.95
❑ MQ45655-5	#38	Karen's Big Lie	$2.95
❑ MQ45654-7	#39	Karen's Wedding	$2.95
❑ MQ47040-X	#40	Karen's Newspaper	$2.95

More Titles...➡

The Baby-sitters Little Sister titles continued...

Available wherever you buy books, or use this order form.

- -

Scholastic Inc., P.O. Box 7502, 2931 E. McCarty Street, Jefferson City, MO 65102

Please send me the books I have checked above. I am enclosing $_____
(please add $2.00 to cover shipping and handling). Send check or money order - no cash or C.O.D.s please.

Name_____ Birthdate_____

Address _____

City_____ State/Zip _____

Please allow four to six weeks for delivery. Offer good in U.S.A. only. Sorry, mail orders are not available to residents to
Canada. Prices subject to change.

BLS495